For Jon and Jamie
—H.Z.

For Stephen
—E.K.

Text copyright © 2006 by Harriet Ziefert
Illustrations copyright © 2006 by Elliot Kreloff
CIP Data is available.
Published in the United States 2006 by
Blue Apple Books
515 Valley Street, Maplewood, N.J. 07040
www.blueapplebooks.com

Distributed in the U.S. by Chronicle Books
First Edition
Printed in China

ISBN 13: 978-1-59354-147-7
ISBN 10: 1-59354-147-3

1 3 5 7 9 10 8 6 4 2

Bigger Than Daddy

Harriet Ziefert   Pictures by Elliot Kreloff

blue Apple Books

Edward was small.
He wanted to be big.

"Daddy, look at me!"
he shouted.
"I'm BIG.
Bigger than you."

"I'm looking at
how big you are,"
said Daddy.
"But I don't want you to fall.
Be careful."

"Look!" Edward shouted. "I'm an airplane. I'm taking off.

ZOOM! ZOOM!

I'm flying!"

"Time for you to fly this way," said Daddy.
"We need to go home for dinner."

Edward zoomed out of the playground.
He waited for his daddy at the corner.
When the light turned green, they crossed.

"I wish I were

tall-

as tall as a tree,"
said Edward.

"You'll be tall someday,"
said Daddy,
"but not as tall
as a tree."

"Look," said Edward. "A fire truck!

I can run *fast* — as fast as a speeding truck."

Edward slowed down and let his daddy catch him.

"Gotcha, Edward!" said Daddy.

"Will you carry me?" asked Edward.

"Okay," answered Daddy. "But I thought you wanted to be big."

"I AM BIG!" said Edward.

"We're home," said Daddy.

Edward ran ahead so he could push the elevator button.

"Can we play
a game
before dinner?"
Edward asked.

until he was under a table.

Edward yelled,
"Come out, Daddy!
Come out
where I can
see you!"

Daddy crawled out from under the table.

"You've been a bad boy!" said Edward. "And you haven't finished your juice."

"I'll drink it,"
said Daddy.

"I'm really thirsty," said Edward.
"May I have a glass of lemonade?"

"I can't get you a drink," answered Daddy.
"I'm too little!"

"But I NEED a drink!" said Edward.
"And I'm hungry."

"I'm too little," insisted Daddy. "I'm too little to fix dinner!"

"Okay," said Edward.
"No more pretending.
You be DADDY and I'll be EDWARD."

Daddy stood up, big and tall.
"All right," he said. "No more pretending.
I'll get you a drink, and dinner
will be ready in ten minutes."

After dinner,
Edward took a bath.

"What if I were a big, huge whale
and swam across the ocean?"
asked Edward.

"If you were a whale
and swam across the ocean,"
said Daddy,
"then how could I . . .

tuck you in . . .

and kiss you good night."